Brewster the Rooster

Written by
Devin Scillian

Illustrated by
Lee White

Sleeping Bear Press™
310 North Main Street, Suite 300
Chelsea, MI 48118
www.sleepingbearpress.com

© 2007 Thomson Gale, a part of the Thomson Corporation.

Thomson, Star Logo and Sleeping Bear Press are trademarks
and Gale is a registered trademark used herein under license.

Printed and bound in the United States.

First Edition

10 9 8 7 6 5 4 3 2 1

Library of Congress Cataloging-in-Publication Data

Scillian, Devin.

Brewster the rooster / written by Devin Scillian ; illustrated by Lee White.
p. cm.
Summary: When Brewster, a prize-winning rooster, suddenly begins crowing at the
most unexpected times, the family tries to figure out what is causing his problem.
ISBN 13: 978-1-58536-311-7
ISBN 10: 1-58536-311-1
[1. Roosters—Fiction. 2. Vision—Fiction.
3. Stories in rhyme.] I. White, Lee, 1970- ill. II. Title.
PZ8.3.S3953Br 2007
[E]—dc22   2006027048

For Pam, with much love.
I never expected such a marvelous friendship.

~Devin

✳

To my brother, Kirk.

~Lee

Brewster the rooster
crowed at the sun
and woke the
whole farm every day.

Farther from here
folks could hear
that rooster
from four farms away.

Off like a siren
he'd hoot and he'd wail,
flapping his wings
with great flair.

His championship cries
won the blue ribbon prize
each year
at the Kansas State Fair.

So life would begin
on the Macintosh farm
the same noisy way
every morning.

He was fit as a fiddle,
but little by little,
he began to crow
without warning.

"I'm worried about Brewster,"
Magnolia said,
mixing carrot cake batter
with raisins.

"Something has changed.
It seems so strange,
but he's crowing at the
oddest occasions."

It was true,
it was true,
the whole family thought.
The rooster had gotten unruly.

Like when Fanny and Paul
were tossing the ball
with Abner, Topper,
and Julie.

Just as young Topper
got ready to throw,
old Brewster crowed
loudly with glee.

It took Topper's breath,
scared him to death,
and the ball got
stuck in a tree.

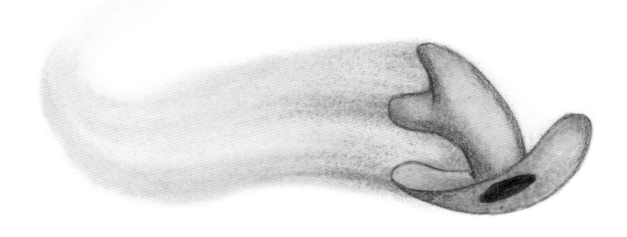

Or that windy day when Zeb climbed the ladder
to paint the old barn red.
With his bucket and pail, a really stiff gale
blew the hat right off his bald head.

Old Brewster let loose with his roosterly roar
and Zeb felt the old ladder quiver.
The west wind blew, and off he flew,
spraying paint all the way to the river.

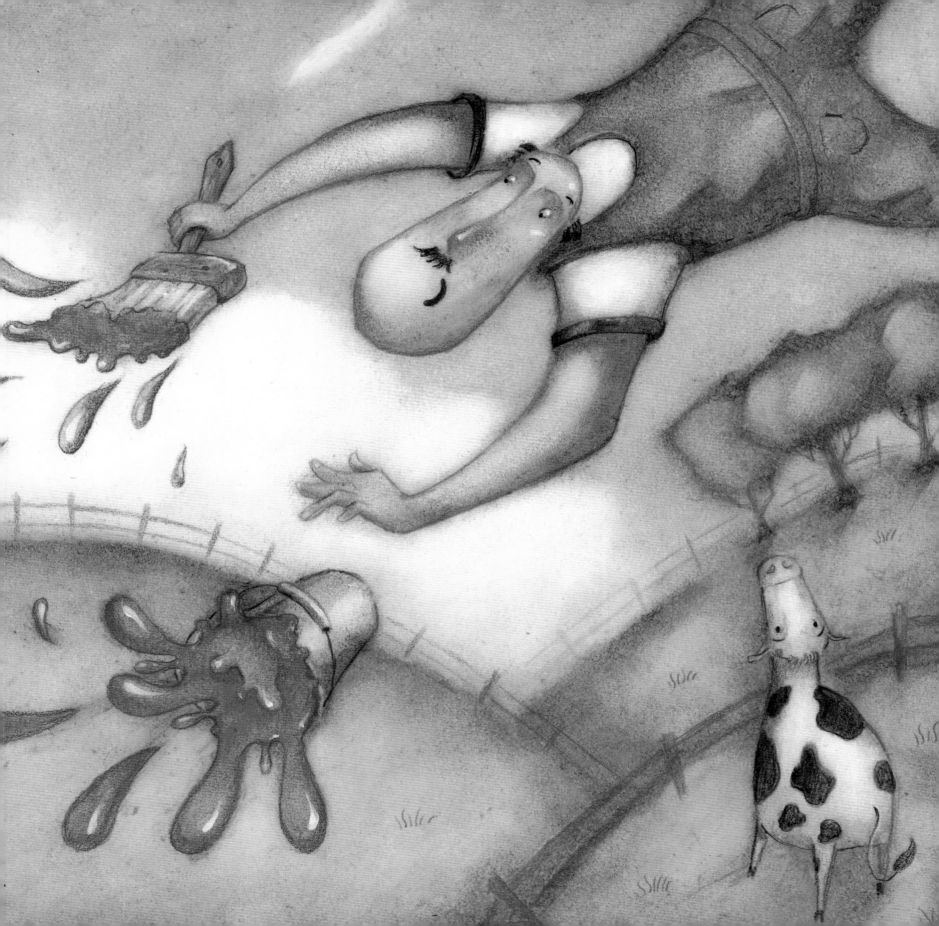

And Grandma Pearl
was down in the kitchen.
It was awful
how they would find her.

While she was cooking,
no one was looking
when Brewster strolled up
behind her.

She was there at the stove,
flipping a hotcake
when Brewster sent
the old woman reeling.

She shrieked at the sound,
started slipping around,
and got batter
all over the ceiling.

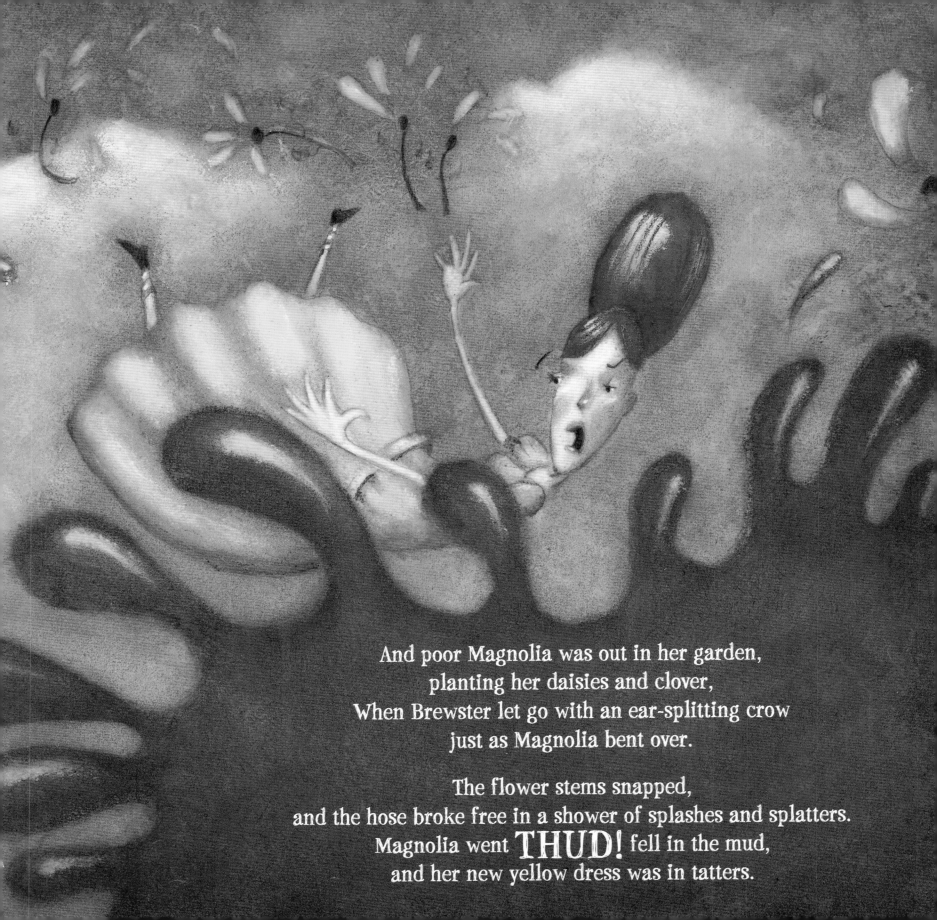

And poor Magnolia was out in her garden,
planting her daisies and clover,
When Brewster let go with an ear-splitting crow
just as Magnolia bent over.

The flower stems snapped,
and the hose broke free in a shower of splashes and splatters.
Magnolia went **THUD!** fell in the mud,
and her new yellow dress was in tatters.

So the family took Brewster to see Doc Sawyer,
who had helped them time and again.
He flipped on his light, which was awfully bright,
and just as the doctor leaned in,

Brewster let loose with his

Cock-a-doodle-doo!

right in Doc Sawyer's good ear.
The doc took a fall, smacked his head on the wall,
and Zeb said, "That's why we're here."

Doc Sawyer stood up and dusted his trousers
and looked Brewster right in the eye.
"I doubt it's contagious, but it's most outrageous.
Any idea as to why?"

Magnolia thought fever, Zeb said a virus,
Abner said, "It's weather connected."
Grandma said flu, Paul thought so, too,
but Fanny thought his feathers were infected.

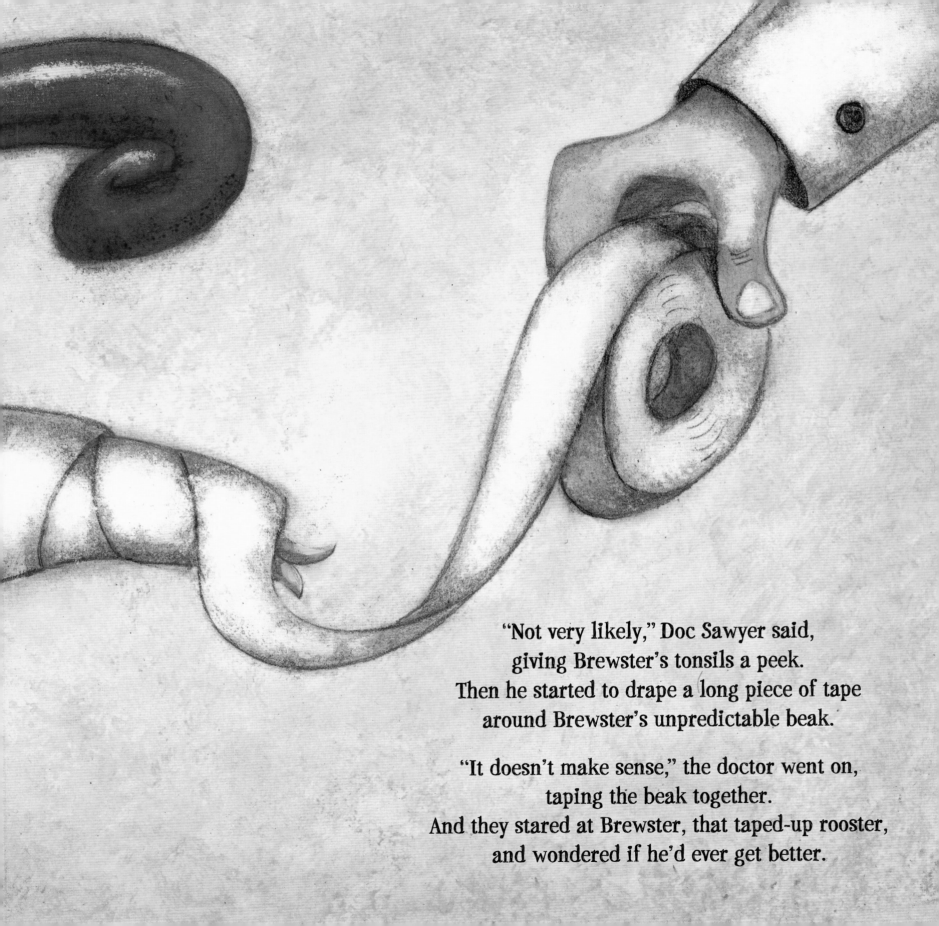

"Not very likely," Doc Sawyer said,
giving Brewster's tonsils a peek.
Then he started to drape a long piece of tape
around Brewster's unpredictable beak.

"It doesn't make sense," the doctor went on,
taping the beak together.
And they stared at Brewster, that taped-up rooster,
and wondered if he'd ever get better.

"He needs glasses,"
little Julie said.

Julie was the youngest and often ignored,
and the family giggled with doubt.
They hee-ed and they hawed and outright guffawed
'til Doc Sawyer said, "Let's hear her out."

"It's simple," said Julie. "It makes perfect sense.
You go ahead and make fun.
But everyone knows that a rooster crows
when he thinks he sees the sun."

Fig. 1

Julie pointed at Doc Sawyer's lamp,
and said, "It has to be the right shape."
She turned on the light, big, round, and bright,
and Brewster tried to crow through the tape.

Fig. 2

Fig. 3

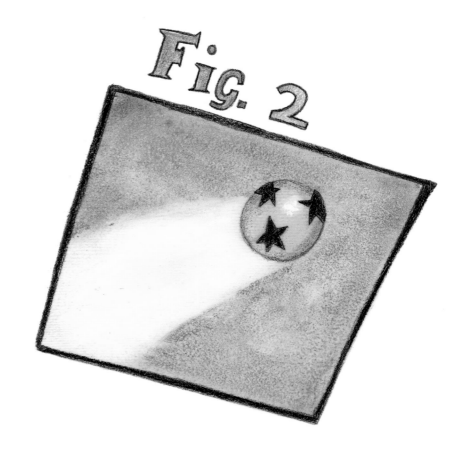

She said, "Think of a ball up in the sky,
or a flapjack round and flat.
Look at Pa from behind and I think that you'll find
he's shiny when he has no hat."

The Macintosh family looked at each other,
and they saw Zeb's knees start to buckle.
They began to smile, and in a short while,
those smiles turned into a chuckle.

Little Julie said, as the laughter grew,
"Ma, when you're planting your clover,
I'd wear a little less of that bright yellow dress
if you're going to be out bending over."

Magnolia laughed until she cried, and said,
"Our rooster has imperfect vision!"
"Lucky for you," the doc said on cue,
"I'm also a rooster optician!"

They gathered 'round Julie and gave her a hug
and told her she sure was smart.
And while smiles were shared, Brewster stared
at the letters on Doc Sawyer's chart.

"Which way does it go?" the doctor would ask,
and Brewster would point a description.
Then they made a stop at the optical shop
to fill Brewster the rooster's prescription.

So now all's well on the Macintosh farm,
and that's the way it should stay.
Now that old Brewster, the spectacled rooster,
crows at just one sunrise a day.

Devin Scillian

Devin Scillian is an award winning author, journalist, and musician. He's the author of the national bestseller *A is for America*. His other titles include *Fibblestax, Cosmo's Moon, P is for Passport* and *One Nation: America by the Numbers*. He currently anchors the news for WDIV-TV, the NBC affiliate in Detroit. Devin, his wife Corey, and their four children live in Grosse Pointe, Michigan. They have a dog, a flop-eared rabbit, a fish, and to their dismay, not one single rooster.

Lee White

Lee White graduated with honors from the prestigious Art Center College of Design in Pasadena, California. Over the years Lee has developed a whimsical style of his own—flying cows, mechanical gizmos, and a whole cast of quirky characters. Realizing his playful style is a perfect fit for children's books, Lee decided to devote his talents to telling stories through images. In addition to illustrating children's books, he also exhibits his art in galleries. *Brewster the Rooster* is Lee's first book with Sleeping Bear Press. He currently lives in Portland, Oregon with his wife, Lisa, and their three crazy cats.